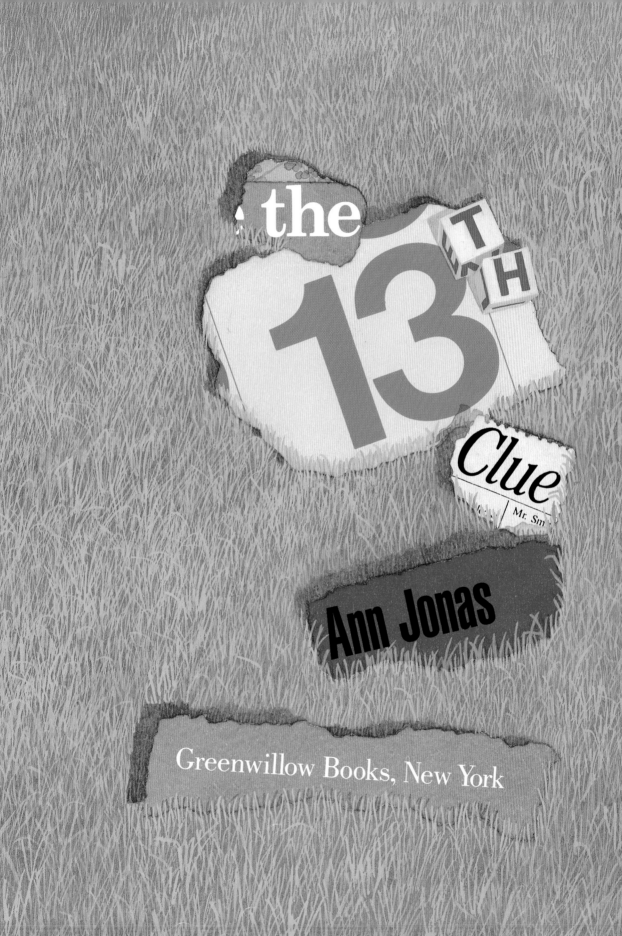

the 13TH
Clue
Mr. Sm

Ann Jonas

Greenwillow Books, New York

September 13,

Dear diary,
    What a terrible
day. No one said
anything at break-
fast and now no one
is even home. At least
they sang to me at

school. That's funny.
The light just went on!

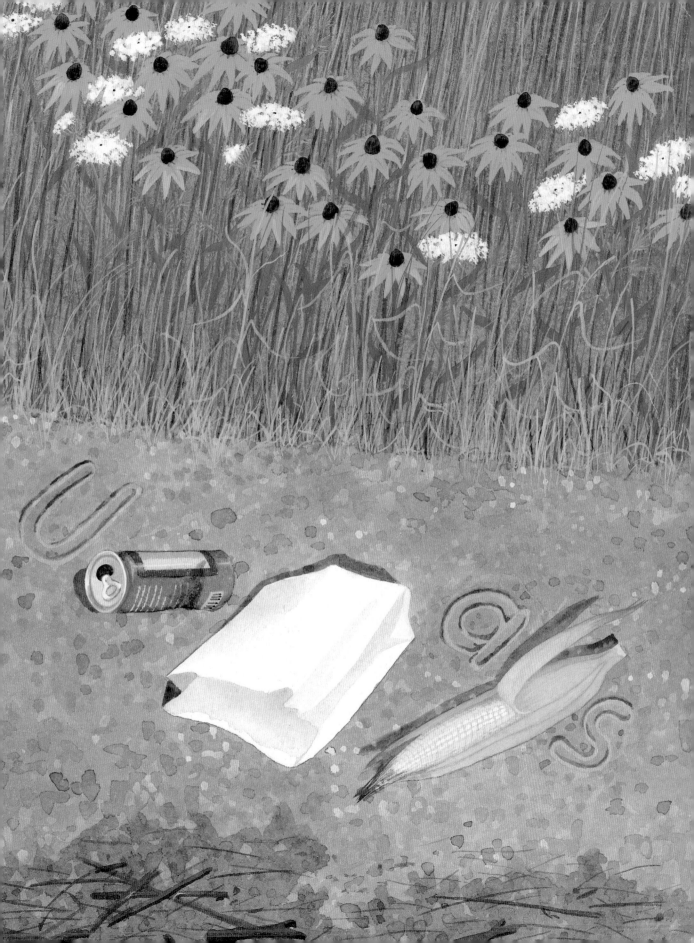

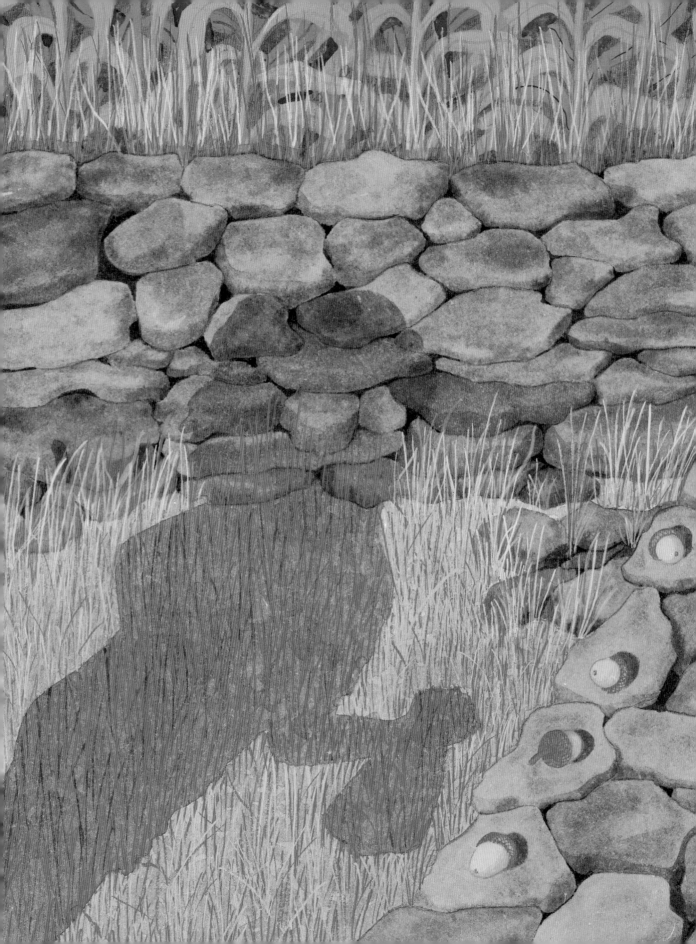

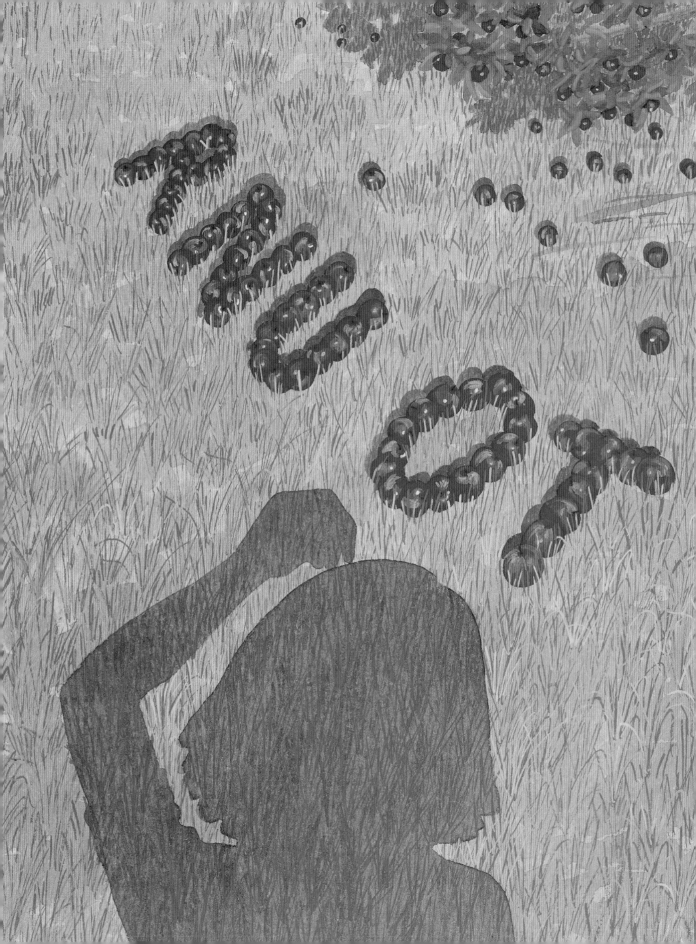

September 13,

Dear diary,
    What a terrible day. No one said anything at breakfast and now no one is even home. At least they sang to me at

school. That's funny.
The light just went on!

What a GREAT
day! They sure
fooled me. That was
the best birthday I
ever had!

THE END

ORF ASUNS CHARSHNIM

Watercolor and gouache paints
were used for the full-color art.

Printed in Hong Kong by South China
Printing Company (1988) Ltd.
First Edition
10 9 8 7 6 5 4 3 2 1

Library of Congress
Cataloging-in-Publication Data
Jonas, Ann.
The 13th clue / by Ann Jonas.
    p.   cm.
Summary: A young girl follows
thirteen clues to a surprise.
ISBN 0-688-09742-1 (trade).
ISBN 0-688-09743-X (lib.)
[1. Birthdays—Fiction.
2. Parties—Fiction.]
I. Title.
II. Title: Thirteenth clue.
PZ7.J664Aaf   1992
[E]—dc20
91-34586   CIP   AC